Top Dog

by Anne Marie Ryan

Illustrated by Vian Oelofsen

Reading Consultant: Susan Nations, M.Ed.

NEW
FOREST
PRESS

Publisher: Tim Cook

Editor: Valerie J. Weber

Designer: Steve West

ISBN: 978 1 84898 505 6

Library of Congress Control Number: 2011924940

U.S. publication © 2011 New Forest Press
Published in arrangement with Black Rabbit Books

PO Box 784, Mankato, MN 56002
www.newforestpress.com

Printed in the USA

15 14 13 12 11 1 2 3 4 5

How to Use This Book

Top Dog is perfect for children who are just starting to learn to read. This book focuses on the sounds *j*, *v*, *w*, *z*, *y*, and *k*.

The Sounds in This Book

Before reading the story, turn to page 24. The grid explains how to pronounce all of the sounds in the story.

Difficult Words

Words in bold in the text do not sound exactly like they look. Children will need help with the difficult part of the word, which is underlined below. The difficult part of the word may not fit the usual rules about what the letter sounds like or the reader may not have learned it yet.

Difficult words in this book:

s<u>ai</u>d   <u>the</u>

To help struggling readers, make flashcards of the difficult words. Ask the reader to find the difficult part within the word, identify the sound, and say the whole word.

"Jed can win," **said** Kim.
"Kip can win," **said** Zak.

"Anna can win," **said** Rob.

The top dog can win a dog kit.

"Is Jed fit?" **said** Val **the** vet.
"Jog, Jed," **said** Kim.

But Jed can not jog.
Anna can!

"Can Kip sit?" **said** Val.

Kip can not sit.
Anna can!

"Can Jed dance?" **said** Val.
"Yes," **said** Kim.

But Jed has a nap.
Anna can dance!

"Kip can beg," **said** Zak.

But Kip bit Val.
Anna can beg.

A cat!

Jed and Kip run!

Anna wins **the** dog kit.

But Jed and Kip had fun!

More about Phonics

Spoken English uses more than 40 speech sounds. Each sound is called a *phoneme*. Some phonemes relate to a single letter (d-o-g) and others to combinations of letters (sh-ar-p). When a phoneme is written down, it is called a *grapheme*. Teaching these sounds, matching them to their written form, and sounding out words for reading is the basis of phonics.

Early phonics instruction gives children the tools to sound out, blend, and say the words without having to rely on memory or guesswork. This instruction gives children the confidence and ability to read unfamiliar words, helping them progress toward independent reading.

About the Consultant

Susan Nations (M.Ed.) is a reading consultant, author, and literacy coach. She is National Board Certified in the area of Literacy and has a Reading Endorsement. Nations has spent more than 25 years working in early education. Currently, she is an intervention teacher and works with students and teachers to implement and improve literacy instruction and acquisition.

A Pronunciation Guide

All of the sounds in this grid are in the story.
The highlighted sounds are the focus of this book.

s as in *sat*	*a* as in *ant*	*t* as in *tin*
p as in *pig*	*i* as *ink*	*n* as in *net*
c as in *cat*	*e* as in *egg*	*h* as in *hen*
r as in *rat*	*m* as in *mug*	*d* as in *dog*
g as in *get*	*o* as in *ox*	*u* as in *up*
l as in *log*	*f* as in *fan*	*b* as in *bag*
j as in *jug*	*v* as in *van*	*w* as in *wet*
z as in *zip*	*y* as in *yet*	*k* as in *kit*

Be careful not to add an *uh* sound to *s, t, p, c, h, r, m, d, g, l, f,* and *b*. For example, say "*fff,*" not "*fuh,*" and "*sss,*" not "*suh.*"